The Story of the Dragon Who Lost His Fire

Authors: Neo Rung and Liv Larsson

Illustrations: Maria Tison-Larsson

Translation: Liv Larsson and Monica Ekneling

www.friareliv.com
www.livlarsson.com

Original title: *Sagan om draken som inte kunde spruta eld*
Authors: Neo Rung and Liv Larsson
Illustrations: Maria Tison-Larsson
Translation: Liv Larsson and Monica Ekneling
Layout: Liz and Rebecca Tencic, Komandå

ISBN: 978-91-87489-90-7

Friare Liv
Mjösjölidvägen 47, SE-946 40 Svensbyn, Sweden
info@friareliv.se
www.friareliv.com

Tekshek is sad. Something terrible has happened. He can no longer breathe fire. No matter how hard he tries, no fire comes out of his mouth. He is standing with his head down, ashamed, and nothing feels fun.

A few days ago, when a few flames were still coming out of his mouth, he told his family. Mom, Dad and his older sister, Timana, all know the awful truth. And now there is no fire at all...

"How are you doing Tekshek?" his mother asks.

"Are you ok?" his father adds.

They see that his head is hanging down sadly.

"I can't do anything, I can't even do something as simple as breathing fire." Tekshek answers quietly.

"I don't feel like a real dragon anymore," says Tekshek looking sadly at his mother.

"Oh sweetheart come on", his mom answers, "It's not the end of the world, we still love you. And it could happen to anyone. You are ok! With or without fire!".

But it doesn't help, however much she tries to encourage him. Tekshek is still as sad as ever.

"I feel pity for the boy, it is not so easy" says Tekshek's father glaring a bit irritated at Teksheks mother.

"Poor boy. I know it's not easy, but I'm sure it will pass," he comforts Tekshek.

But Tekshek doesn't believe him. And it's not comforting, because right now all he wants to do is to breathe fire.

Tekshek's big sister Timana is getting sick of all the talk about not being able to breathe fire. She loudly exclaims,

"Stop whining. Don't behave like a crybaby!"

Then Tekshek gets really sad and leaves with his tail between his legs.

Tekshek's friends, Chorella and Vortan, find him all by himself in the woods.

"Why are you here all by yourself?", asks Chorella.

He tells them the awful story about not having been able to breathe fire for several days. Vortan, who likes to understand things, asks eagerly,

"When did it start?" "How does it feel?" "What have you eaten?" "Do you have a fever?" "Does it hurt anywhere?"

After a while Tekshek becomes totally exhausted from trying to answer all the questions so he asks Vortan to stop.

Chorella, who has been standing beside them in silence, would also like to try to help Tekshek.

"Try to breathe really hard, and maybe it will work? Pull from your toes and don't stop until the fire comes!".

Tekshek, who has already tried everything and doesn't want any more advice, respons with a trembling voice

"Believe me, I've tried EVERYTHING and I know that it's not possible!"

He flies away, leaving his friends a little surprised behind.

Tekshek flies to his grandmother and grandfather in the mountains. They have already heard that he can't breathe fire.

Grandma immediately starts telling a story about a dragon that was her friend when she was small. "The dragon was enchanted by a witch and he couldn't breathe fire after that, and ..."

She continues and Tekshek listens for a while, and then whispers downheartedly to Grandpa,

"No one understands me! They are only giving advice, asking me to be quiet, or trying to encourage or comfort me. No one is really listening!"

17

Grandpa understands.

He hushes Grandma and she immediately gets the hint. She understands that it doesn't help Tekshek to listen to stories right now. For
a while they sit together in silence.

"Do you just want someone to listen to you and understand how hard it is to not be able to breathe fire when you are a dragon?" Grandpa guesses with a soft voice.

It feels so good that someone tries to understand and Tekshek nods.

"Is it also hard to feel like a real dragon without fire?" Grandma gently wonders.

"Yes, exactly". Tekshek says and feels a very strange cold feeling inside of him. He has not felt this until now and he tells Grandma.

After listening to Tekshek for a bit more, she says, "You know Tekshek, I feel a little worried and would like to see if there is anything we can do about this. I wonder if you'd like us to follow you to the doctor and see if she can help?"

Tekshek hesitates a little. It was nice to be with Grandpa and Grandma and to feel the relief that someone was finally listening to him. But still he couldn't breathe fire. And he still feels cold in his heart.

He looks inside and searches his feelings, and then says, "Okay. If you follow me there, we can go!"

So let's listen", says the doctor when they get there. She takes her Stethoscope and listens to Tekshek's heart. (For all of you who don't know – it is from the dragon's special heart that their fire comes).

"Oh!" She says, in surprise, "it seems that part of your heart has frozen to ice".

When Tekshek hears this he gets scared and sad and starts to cry.
Large dragon tears roll down his cheeks. He cries so much that
his dragon wings are trembling.

"What if it never passes, what if my heart is frozen forever!"

The doctor understands that it is important to listen not only with the Stethoscope, but also with her heart. The matter of a frozen dragon heart is very serious. She really tries to connect with how sad this is for Tekshek.

Then she asks to see if she has understood:

"Are you sad because you so badly want to be able to do what is so important for dragons?"

"Yes" Tekshek answers, and cries even more. Now he feels a little bit better since the doctor also seems to understand how terribly sad this is for him.

They sit together like that for a while, crying and talking, and suddenly Tekshek notices something strange. The tears are warm. And they become warmer. And warmer. They even start feeling hot! And even hotter!

"Hot tears?", I have never felt this before. He calls out with surprise. "How is this possible?"

The Doctor becomes curious and takes her Stethoscope and listens to Teksheks heart again. At first she doesn't believe her ears!

"Can this really be true? The heart has melted! The tears must have come from there, when the ice in the heart became water."

But Tekshek has already tried and there is some fire now. First as if from a small match, then as much as from a candle and NOW, real flames, as from a big fire.

"Hooray, I can blow fire!" Tekshek shouts.

""Here comes the fire," cheers Grandma.

"Hooray for the warm heart", grandfather sings.

The doctor smiles, satisfaction showing all over her dragon face.

From that day, dragons know how to cure a frozen heart. It has become widely known in all dragon kingdoms that the best medicine for a dragon who can't breathe fire is to be able to cry.

And that talking about one's feelings with someone, doctor or not doesn't matter, who is listening from their heart, can help keep you warm inside.

And by the way, did you know, that human beings also has frozen hearts sometimes. Maybe this way of listening would be a help for us as well!

Games and questions

What do you think Tekshek's mom was needing when she tried to encourage him? Do you think she wanted:

- Some peace and quiet?
- A sense of belonging?
- To give something?
- To experience more freedom?
- To get support?
- To feel understood?
- Some other need?

What do you think Tekshek was feeling when his mom tried to encourage him?

Worry?	Disappointment?
Joy?	Sadness?
Irritation?	Some other feeling?
Curiosity?	

What do you think Tekshek's father was needing when he was trying to comfort Tekshek?

- Some peace and quiet?
- A sense of belonging?
- To give something?
- To experience more freedom?
- To get support?
- To feel understood?
- Some other need?

What do you think Tekshek was feeling when he was comforted by his father?

Worry?   Disappointment?
Joy?   Sadness?
Irritation?   Some other feeling?
Curiosity?

What could a dragon dad and a dragon mom say to their dragon child instead of giving advice, comfort and encourage them, that would make a difference for a sad dragon child?

Page 9

What do you think Timana was feeling when she called Tekshek a CRYBABY and told him to stop whining?

Worry?   Disappointment?
Joy?   Sadness?
Irritation?   Some other feeling?
Curiosity?

What do you think Timana was needing when she called Tekshek a CRYBABY and told him to stop whining?

- Some peace and quiet?
- A sense of community?
- To give something?
- To get support?
- To feel understood?
- Some other need?

What could Timana have said or done that would have contributed to Tekshek more?

Page 11

What would you do or say to Tekshek if you met him in the forest?

Page 12

What do you think Vortan was feeling when he asked Tekshek all the questions?

Worry?   Disappointment?
Joy?   Sadness?
Irritation?   Some other feeling?
Curiosity?

What do you think Vortan was needing when he asked Tekshek all the questions?

· Some peace and quiet?
· A sense of community?
· To give something?
· To experience more freedom?
· To get support?
· To feel understood?
· Some other need?

Page 13

What do you think Chorella was feeling when she gave Tekshek advice?

Worry?   Disappointment?
Joy?   Sadness?
Irritation?   Some other feeling?
Curiosity?

What do you think Chorella was wanting and needing when she gave Tekshek advice?

- Some peace and quiet?
- A sense of community?
- To give something?
- To experience more freedom?
- To get support?
- To feel understood?
- Some other need?

Page 16

What do you think Grandma was feeling when she began to tell a story when Tekshek came to visit?

Worry?	Disappointment?
Joy?	Sadness?
Irritation?	Some other feeling?
Curiosity?	

What do you think Grandma was wanting with telling a story when Tekshek came to visit?

- Some peace and quiet?
- A sense of community?
- To give something?
- To experience more freedom?
- To get support?
- To feel understood?
- Some other need?

Page 16

What do you think Tekshek was feeling when Grandma told her story?

Worry?   Disappointment?

Joy?   Sadness?

Irritation?   Some other feeling?

Curiosity?

Page 17

What do you think Tekshek was feeling when he said "Nobody listens to me"?

Worry?   Disappointment?

Joy?   Sadness?

Irritation?   Some other feeling?

Curiosity?

What do you think Tekshek was needing?

· Some peace and quiet?
· A sense of community?
· To give something?
· To experience more freedom?
· To get support?
· To feel understood?
· Something else?

Page 18

What do you think Grandpa was needing when he hushed Grandma?

· Some peace and quiet?
· A sense of community?
· To give something?
· To experience more freedom?
· To get support?
· To feel understood?
· Something else?

What do you think Tekshek was feeling when his grandfather listened and tried to understand what was happening within him?

Page 19

Worry?   Disappointment?
Joy?   Sadness?
Irritation?   Some other feeling?
Curiosity?

Why do you think Tekshek wanted Grandma and Grandpa to follow him to the doctor?

Page 22, 27

Do you think there is anything you can hear with your heart that you can't hear with a Stethoscope?

What do you think the doctor was feeling when she listened to Tekshek's heart and noticed that it was melting?

What do you think Tekshek was feeling when flames started to come out of his mouth?

Page 29

Why do you think he felt that way?

Why do you think Grandpa said "Hooray for the warm heart"?

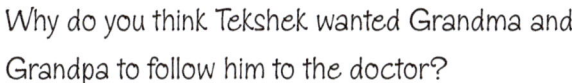
Page 30

Draw a picture of a time when you felt sad, in the same way that Tekshek was.

Draw a picture of a time when you felt relieved and happy.

What would you do if you were a dragon and were unable to breathe fire?

Draw or write.

www.friareliv.com
www.livlarsson.com

www.ingramcontent.com/pod-product-compliance
Lightning Source LLC
Chambersburg PA
CBHW051601120626
46551CB00013B/1621